The Tale Of
SYBIL
THE SQUIRREL

Written and Illustrated by
Michael Quinlyn-Nixon

**Grosvenor House
Publishing Limited**

The Queen's Platinum
Jubilee
5 June 2022
Best wishes
M Quinlyn-Nixon

This book is published by
Grosvenor House Publishing Ltd
Link House
140 The Broadway, Tolworth, Surrey, KT6 7HT.
www.grosvenorhousepublishing.co.uk

A CIP record for this book
is available from the British Library

ISBN 978-1-83975-696-2

Dedicated to my two wonderful sisters,
Susan and Sarah, who are very special to me,
and my long-term friend Sara Oldham in Carlisle, Cumbria.

"It is more difficult to take a specific path –
when you're not 'invited' on that journey".

Michael Quinlyn-Nixon • 23 February 2016

Appearances are only skin deep,
look past all of that -
just take a peek...

I started writing this children's book with the aim of addressing some of the issues I experienced and witnessed whilst as a child at school. Sadly, the world has not changed much since then and there is still so much bullying, intimidation and victimisation going on in our children's lives. I hope that this book will make some children (and their parents) realise how damaging this can be and how important it is to treat everyone with dignity, equality and respect.

I also hope that this book will encourage people to value others, despite their differences, and see each and every person as a 'unique and precious individual'. This one book cannot tackle all of these issues, obviously, but even a 'drop in the ocean' is better than nothing.

It was back in 1996-97, when I was living and working in Carlisle, that I came up with the idea of a book about a purple squirrel. It stayed on the 'back-burner' of my mind for many years; it is nice to think that at the time of writing this note that it is nearing completion. I hope you, the reader, will like this tale of a quirky and very unique squirrel.

In this tale, Sibyl meets a diva frog, a tactless duckling and a grumpy hedgehog, all of whom eventually come to realise that outward appearances are only skin deep and that the true value of someone is not what they look like or what they own, but the nature of their kindness and willingness to help others. Sibyl is a character with a heart-of-gold, which is **much more** precious than a glittery heart-shaped gemstone!

Writing this book and creating the illustrations took seven-months, so I sincerely hope that the time and effort will prove worth it and that you and your children and grandchildren will come to enjoy this book more and more with every occasion you read it...

M Quinlyn-Nixon

21st April 2021

Have you spotted all the ladybirds (pardon the pun)?
There are a great many ladybirds dotted about this book, I wonder how many you can find. Oh, and don't forget the one on the cover!

I would like you to have
a very quick think...
Have you ever seen an elephant
whose skin was **pink?**

Have you ever spotted a large gnu,
whose bottom was a shade of
blue?

There's one tall animal I bet you haven't
seen - a giraffe with patches that are
green!

This tale is not about an
animal in a zoo,
but, she was still an
unusual colour too...

Iris

6

Gnorman

To find out more you really should,
follow me to...
        Wriggly Wood.

You can hop or run, fly or crawl...
    and that invitation is open to all.

So, please turn the page and make a
start to hear about an animal with a

very special heart...

Sybil is the main character
    in this storybook,
    but, something is different
    about her - just take a look...

She's a purple squirrel with a
    large **bushy tail;**
she's actually lilac
    (that's a purple that's pale).

No squirrel this colour
    had ever been seen!
She might as well have been
    blue, pink or green!

Because of this the other
    animals were so unfair...
about Sybil's feelings
    they did not care.

The only friend Sybil had
    was Doug-Down the mole,
she would chat to him
    next to his round mole-hole.

None of the other animals
    were so kind and good,
so, Sybil had no other friends
    in Wriggly Wood!

One day, Sybil went
for a little stroll...
she was going to visit
Doug-Down the mole.

Amongst the bluebells
Sybil skipped and hopped,
Then, up out of the grass
a green head popped!

It was Marsha, the frog,
and she was about to cry...
her puddle had gone
and her skin was quite dry.

If this worried little frog
didn't get water soon
her skin would wrinkle in the sun
- just like a prune!

Sybil thought quick and then
Sybil thought fast...
And she came up with an idea
at last!

She would shake the rain
  off the leaves of an oak...
the raindrops would fall
  to earth - the frog to soak.

So, up the tree she quickly
  leapt and dashed...
she shook the wet leaves and
  ...the rain water splashed!

Down below the droplets of rain
  soaked the happy frog...
the ground became muddy
  until it was a tiny bog.

Sybil said, "Marsha, I am so
  pleased that idea did work",
but the vain frog turned away
  - with a shoulder jerk!

Sybil stood there and really
  couldn't quite understand...
Why was Marsha so rude, when
  she had given her a hand?

Quietly, Sybil just turned
  around and walked away...
To leave Marsha, alone,
  in her pond to play.

Quite a while later,
Sybil leapt from tree to tree.
It was wonderful to feel
so alive and free!

But, far down below the branches
she heard a sad 'quack'
and saw a fluffy, little duckling
lying flat on his back.

There he was with a small
boot stuck on his head!
To a little duckling
it was as heavy as lead!

His name was Bob
and he was stuck!
This shouldn't happen
...to a duck.

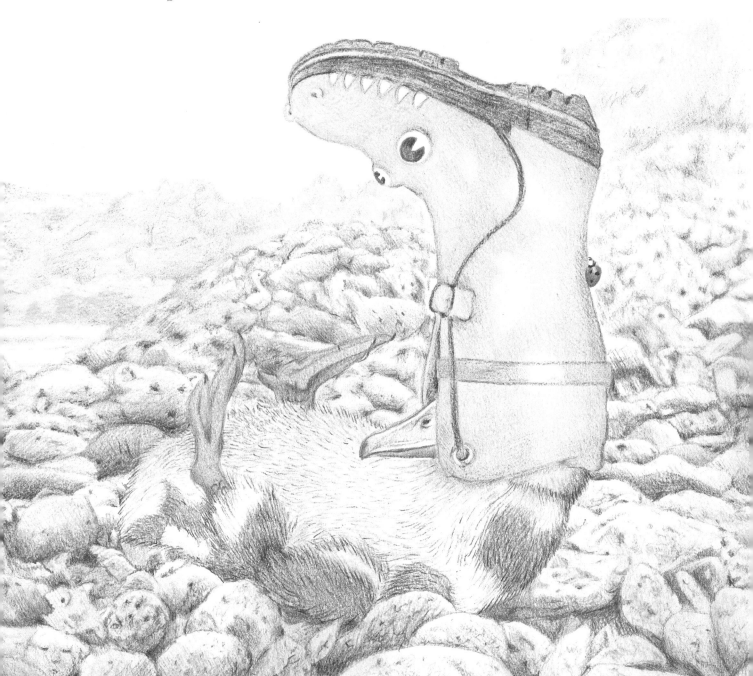

Sybil said, "I will try and help you out!" She tugged hard at the boot, which made Bob shout!

But Sybil still pulled and tugged with all her might. Oh, my goodness, it was stuck tight!

Then off came the boot with a great big yank. It landed on the riverbank...

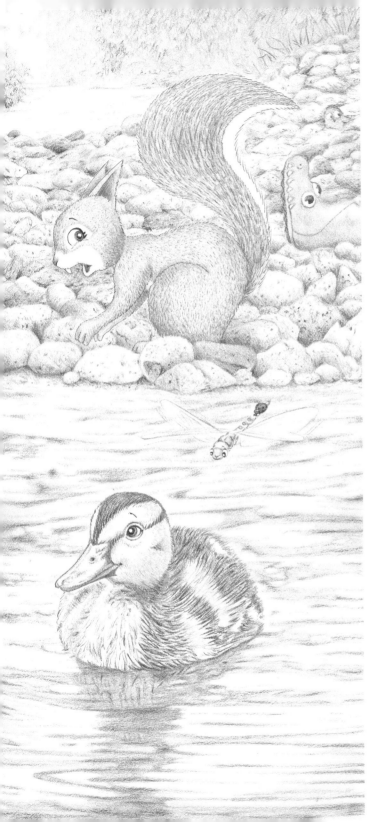

Thanks, was what Bob
was about to say...
but, his face lost its smile
and it turned...quite grey.

He said, "Oh dear, your lilac
fur is very strange,
if I were you I'd make a change!"

He waddled into the river
without even a
'thanks' or a 'quack'...
He didn't even take one look back.

Sybil thought, but I am happy
just being me...
Then she quickly ran up
the nearest tall tree.

But, as she leapt and
capered through the wood,
she tried to forget what Bob
had said; she wished she could...

As she got nearer to the hole,
    belonging to her friend Doug,
she saw a...
        ...very happy bug.

The bug was leaping
up and down with delight...
he had just escaped
from an awful fright!

He had just been sitting down
to have a nice cuppa...
when a hedgehog had wanted
him for her supper!

But, just as the hedgehog
was about to take a bite...
something fell from the sky
that was large and white.

Sybil took a quick look around
    something white and lumpy
    lay on the ground!

It was Hodge the hedgehog
    stuck inside a plastic bag;
it had caught on her prickles
    - such a snag.

Hodge was grumpy and she
    groaned and she kicked.
Sybil had to be careful
    in case she got pricked!

Sybil said, "I will see
    if I can help".
Inside the carrier bag,
    Hodge gave out a yelp!

Sybil very carefully got
    Hodge out...
"Thank goodness!",
    the hedgehog did shout.

But, when Hodge saw it was
Sybil who had 'saved the day'
she turned around and
just walked away!

Sybil thought, in this wood
there are these trends,
it seems a **struggle**
to make new friends!

The next day, all the animals
    were happy and carefree...
it was their annual party
    from Great Oak, the tree.

But they would have to wait
    a few more hours...
playing hide and seek
    amongst the flowers.

Sybil went for a
    lonely little walk;
there was no one to play with
    or even to talk.

But, as she wandered she saw
    a distant glint;
Sybil had to shield her eyes
    and squint.

Something had glittered
    in the light of the sun,
oh, something exciting
    she thought has begun...

There on a rock was
    a jewel ~ so shiny!
It was quite big and not so tiny...

It was the most beautiful
    heart-shaped jewel!
It was enough to make you drool.

When all the animals
saw her shiny prize...
they couldn't quite
believe their eyes!

Because of her jewel,
Sybil was now everyone's 'friend',
someone on whom they could depend.

But, Sybil really was
no one's fool:
they were her friends
just because of the jewel!

Then all the animals sat in a circle
around Great Oak,
and all of them listened
when the great tree spoke...

"This year, I have had to choose
an animal that's made some news!"
The animals all turned and stared at Sybil,
Was Great Oak talking about
this lilac squirrel?

Yes, it was Sybil's name that Great Oak read;
the animals all turned around and said...
"Was she chosen because of her
new shiny glitter?
Because it has set the wood a-twitter?"

reat Oak replied, "Beauty
and wealth all play their part,
but, they cannot beat
a loving heart!"

The animals all bowed
their heads with shame;
they knew they were
the ones to blame.

Great Oak said, "Sybil has been set apart
because of her kind, forgiving heart".

So, all of the animals said sorry
- each one took their turn,
and said because of their mistakes
they would learn...

And even grumpy Hodge said
she would make a start -
to have a more caring heart.

Then they all danced and played fun games,
there was no more 'calling names'!

So, all the animals went to sleep
at the end of that day,
having enjoyed an evening of
friendship and play.

- The End -

A word about the illustrations:
The thirty illustrations were created over a period of seven-months and this time included the book layout and writing the poem. A great many coloured-pencils and watercolour paints were used to create the illustrations, which I wanted to have a pastel-like look to them. Designing the character of Sybil the Squirrel has taken quite a long time; I was so fussy about how I wanted this character to look. Thank you to my 'unnamed friends' who inspired me to create the characters of Hodge, Marsha and Den.

I would like to acknowledge these people and companies for their various forms of support and encouragement. Thank you…

Maddy

Mary

Milly

Thank you to all my family and friends, who have given me encouragement over the years with regard to my art (you know who you are), to Mary Lupton, Marie L. Smyth, Robert and Carole Nixon whom I shared my ideas with and who provided support for this book to be written. A big 'thank you' must go to my "Creative Art Directors", namely Neil W. Donnelly for his great insight into art, books and illustrations and Lesley A. Doogan for all my 'technical requirements'. I am extremely grateful to you for your ideas, suggestions and continued support.

Thank you also to Vincent J. McSherry, Cherry D. Balme, Vicky Boddy, Louise A. Hobson and Jennifer A. Stephenson for listening to my frequent art/writing frustrations and questions!
Thank you to Marie Matthewson, from Learning for Life, who kindly offered to proof-read my book.
Thank you to Grosvenor House Publishing Ltd. for the support they have provided to get this book published.
Thank you to Helene M. Phillips for all her help in providing written profiles for my art and graphic literature.
Thank you to the young people, including: Daphne, Lily and Remy, who modelled for the illustration on page 8.

ABOUT THE AUTHOR AND ILLUSTRATOR

Michael Quinlyn-Nixon, an artist and author born-and-bred in the North East of England, has been producing a wide range of illustrations in watercolour and coloured-pencil since his first exhibition in April 1988.

Michael, who was born in Blackhill, Consett, has enjoyed drawing since he was a child and his talent was nurtured at Tanfield School in Stanley, Derwentside College in Consett, New College Durham and Cumbria Institute of the Arts in Carlisle - where he studied graphic design. Michael has been employed in the areas of marketing and retail, as well as the newspaper, educational and specialist learning industries.

Michael's illustrations became known to an international audience with his popular *Bear-a-thought* limited-edition greeting cards and calendars. His first calendar was produced in **2002** - the centenary of the teddy bear - and his work has won him a great many admirers from as far as Durban to Denmark and Quebec to Queensland.

In **2020**, Michael wrote and illustrated his first-ever publication, *The Tale of the Vampire Rabbit*, which has received some glowing reviews and media coverage for both his illustrations and his writing.

His work often reflects his love of natural history and, because of his attention to detail, requires a great deal of vision, commitment and above all…patience!

Helene M. Phillips

3

"I might never be at 'the top of the tree' -
but it won't stop me climbing the branches".
Michael Quinlyn-Nixon • 10 July 2020